GRANDMA
and
GRANDPA'S
GARDEN

Neil Griffiths

ILLUSTRATED BY
Gabriella Buckingham

Lucy loved to visit her grandma and grandpa. They lived in a little country cottage with a beautiful, big garden.

Grandma and Grandpa loved being together in
their garden more than anywhere else and could
almost always be found there, busily digging,
weeding, pruning and planting.

They loved it too when their granddaughter Lucy visited, as she was always so helpful and interested.

Grandma liked to be amongst the flower beds most of all, whilst Grandpa was always his happiest in the vegetable patch.

Grandma grew flowers of every kind – floppy daisies, tall lupins, giant sunflowers and tiny forget-me-nots.

But her favourite flowers were her roses. She loved their colours, delicate petals and wonderful scent.

Grandpa grew vegetables of every kind in the straightest of rows – carrots, cabbages and beetroot, enormous bendy marrows and long runner beans.

They were often in the garden together all day, from sunrise to dusk, stopping only for a chat over a cup of tea and a slice of Grandma's delicious fruitcake.

Grandpa would tell Grandma how glorious her flowers were looking and Grandma would admire Grandpa's wonderful vegetables.

They were so happy together, and even happier when Lucy came to stay and help. They taught her how to plant seeds, care for young seedlings, prune, weed and harvest the fresh vegetables and flowers.

However, these long, happy days did not last forever. Sadly, Grandma became very ill. She was so poorly that she had to stay in bed and couldn't go out into their much-loved garden.

Grandpa moved their bed towards the window so Grandma could see her wonderful flowers. He also cut her a fresh bunch each day and placed them in a vase next to her. There she could smell their fragrant scent.

It was there, one quiet morning, that Grandma took a last look at her beloved garden, smiled, closed her eyes and passed away in Grandpa's gentle arms.

Lucy was unable to visit
Grandpa for several
weeks. Her mum said
she should wait a while.

When she finally did, she was
so sad to find Grandpa sitting
quietly on the verandah
rocking in his chair.

The garden too looked sad, with weeds creeping amongst the flowers and vegetables that had dried and withered. Grandpa told Lucy that he felt too sad to go into the garden, as he was missing Grandma so much. Lucy stared quietly into the neglected garden.

"But Grandpa," she suddenly said, "doesn't the garden remind you of the happy times with Grandma?" Grandpa still looked sad. Lucy held Grandpa's hand gently. "Look, don't the roses remind you of Grandma's rosy cheeks?" she whispered. Grandpa smiled slightly.

"And look, the forget-me-nots
are as blue as Grandma's eyes."
Grandpa's smile got wider.

"What about the sunflowers? They remind me of Grandma's smile. I can almost see Grandma now," she beamed. By now, Grandpa had tears of happiness in his eyes and he hugged Lucy.

"You're right. I can see Grandma too!" he smiled. "Come on, we've work to do!"

Lucy spent all her spare time over the following years, planting and caring for the garden with Grandpa.

Late one evening, as dusk fell, Lucy and Grandpa sat on the verandah with a cup of cocoa, tired, but pleased with their day's work. After a quiet moment together, Lucy said. "Grandpa, the garden will always remind me of you too."